Night Sounds, Morning Colors

NIGHT SOUNDS, MORNING COLORS

Rosemary Wells *pictures by* David McPhail

Dial Books for Young Readers New York

To Amy and Cynthia Glidden
R. W.

For Rosemary — who saw the way long before I did
D. M.

Published by Dial Books for Young Readers
A Division of Penguin Books USA Inc.
375 Hudson Street
New York, New York 10014

Designed by Jane Byers Bierhorst
Printed in the U.S.A.
First Edition
10 9 8 7 6 5 4 3 2 1

Library of Congress Cataloging in Publication Data

Wells, Rosemary.
Night sounds, morning colors / Rosemary Wells
pictures by David McPhail. — 1st ed.
p. cm.
Summary / A child explores the
senses by reflecting on experiences
associated with the seasons.
ISBN 0-8037-1301-0 (trade)
ISBN 0-8037-1302-9 (library)
[1. Senses and sensation — Fiction.
2. Seasons — Fiction.] I. McPhail,
David M., ill. II. Title.
PZ7.W46843Ni 1994 [E] — dc20
93-31815 CIP AC

The art for this book
was rendered in acrylic paints.

When I Wake Up

Outside my window
there is a morning mist, hiding everything
but a big droopy spiderweb
loaded with emerald raindrops.

At breakfast the sun appears through the clouds suddenly.
It shines right into the stream of gold honey
that spins from my spoon to my biscuit.

In the morning I garden with my mother.
The violets we plant are so bright
in their deep black earth
that my mother is sure they are laughing and singing.
She washes my hands.

I watch Jim, our goldfish,
weave in and out the windows of his pagoda.
My father cuts fruits of four colors for my lunch.

After lunch my sister dances the tango for me.

Night Sounds

After supper Grandpa reads to me.
His quiet voice rolls up and down like ocean waves.

Through the screen door I hear the rain
pattering and popping on the leaves outside.
My mother makes me an egg-cup ice cream sundae.
The spoon clinks against the china.
The chocolate sauce sounds thick and sleepy.

Next I listen to my mother's footsteps
tapping down the hallway. She runs my bath.
The water gushes into the tub.

After my bath my father turns out the light
and hums "Danny Boy" to me.

Through my window drift the night songs
of creatures I can't see.
They whirr and hoot and chuckle and click.

Far away I can hear a train come and go.
Its whistle mixes with the wind.

In My Kitchen

Grandma takes me to the bakery.
The whole store smells of new, warm bread.
She buys poppy seed rolls, my mother's favorite.
The baker gives me a pumpkin cookie.
It tastes of Halloween.

Next door we buy roses for my mother's birthday.
While Grandma decides, she lets me hold her wallet.
Creaky, strong, and worn shiny,
it has the secret smell of old leather.

When we get home, Grandma makes a birthday cake.
All around the stove is a zone
of vanilla and butter and chocolate.

When the cake is done, Grandma opens a new bag of Kentucky Kitchen coffee. "It's the kind *my* grandmother bought," she tells me. "Breathe it in and smell the mountains of home."

Everyone kisses my mother at her birthday dinner.
Her flowers have opened in the warm air,
and they fill the room with sweetness.

My mother puts me to bed.
I smell of clean towels and soap.
She smells just of herself.

Winter Walk

My brother wants to look for a ball he lost
this summer behind the hill.
He tells me to wear my thick woolly sweater
and my heavy socks.

Bingo comes with us.

A gust of freezing wind blows right through my hair.
I pick an icicle. It is almost sharp,
but the point melts in my hand.

We go through a pine grove.
Under our feet there are a million dry needles,
spongy and springy as a mattress.

Suddenly I walk right into a prickly bush.
A thorn rips through my pants and cuts me, and I cry.
My brother hugs me.

He gives me a feather
he says is from a dove's wing.
He runs its velvety softness along my cheek.

We cannot find the ball.
I have a hard, cold stone in my sock.

My cut stings and my sweater itches.
My brother carries me home.

He makes me hot toast

with smooth shivering jelly on top.

I lie on the sunny window seat.
Next to me lies Bingo. Her warm tummy is softer even than the dove's feather, softer than sleep.